The Magic Key

The Cream Cake Mystery

OXFORD

UNIVERSITY PRESS

Mum and the children were walking home from school. Chip was worried – he had to write a rap for his homework, so Nadim said he'd help him.

'I'll start you off and you do the next line,' said Nadim. 'Chip's my name. Rapping's my . . .' he began.

'Homework?' said Chip.

'No,' cried Nadim. 'Why can't you work out what comes next?'

Floppy rolled his eyes, it was so obvious. It's 'Rapping's my game!' he thought. I wish they could hear me!

The key on Floppy's collar started to glow.

Suddenly Nadim, Chip, and Floppy were dragged into a vortex of beautiful colours and lights. They were whizzing round and round, faster and faster . . .

They found themselves in a police station, where the superintendent was standing at the counter. Just then, the door opened and a policeman walked in, leading a woman into the station. 'Cassie's her name, stealing's her game,' he said.

The superintendent looked pleased. 'With Jake Blake, there's no mistake,' he said to Chip and Nadim, and then pointed to a pair of police helmets. 'Constables, helmets on!' he told them. 'You! Check out Cream Cake Cassie's records,' he said to Nadim. 'You! Take the sniffer dog and visit the scene of the crime!' he said to Chip.

Floppy was pleased. A nice job for once! he thought.

Chip and Floppy went along to the bakery. 'So, er, what can you tell me about the robbery?' Chip asked the baker.

'Nothing much,' the baker replied. 'This maniac burst in, chanting poetry, and took all my doughnuts!'

Floppy sniffed around and found a torn piece of paper. Chip bent down and took it from him. 'Look at this! It's a poem,' said Chip excitedly. 'The Robber's Rap!'

'The robber must have dropped it when he ran off,' the baker said. 'Well done, officer!'

Back at the station, Nadim had made a discovery too. 'Excuse me, sir. I've checked Cassie's record,' Nadim told Jake Blake. 'And I'm sure she's not the thief!'

All eyes turned to Nadim. 'It's not her normal pattern,' he explained. 'Cream Cake Cassie only steals cream cakes!'

The superintendent was disappointed. 'It looks like we've got the wrong person,' he said.

'Too right, mate!' said Cassie, and walked out of the room.

But Chip had some evidence that might help catch the real robber. 'The robber is a rapper,' he said, holding up the piece of paper.

'Give me your lollies, give me your sweets,' read Nadim. 'Give me your licky, sticky treats!'

'Exactly what the robber said at the Sweet Shop Stick-Up!' Jake gasped.

'You're right – which means . . .' the superintendent started.

'HE must be the robber!' said Jake, pointing at Nadim.

Nadim shook his head. 'No, no! It's written…' he started protesting.

'Yes – in YOUR handwriting!' said Jake, snatching the paper and throwing it in the bin.

'That's not true!' cried Nadim – but it was too late. Jake Blake reached for his handcuffs and put them on Nadim.

'You've got to help me, Chip!' Nadim shouted. 'Find the rhyming pattern and you'll find the crook!'

Floppy retrieved the paper from the bin and passed it to Chip, who looked at it carefully.

'Doughnuts next,' he read. 'And then I'll take a huge, delicious…' But he couldn't read the end.

Floppy barked. It was so obvious to him, but he couldn't get Chip to understand. Chip thought hard, 'a huge, delicious…sparkling lake!' he cried.

Chip shook his head. 'Well, it rhymes, but it doesn't make much sense,' he said.

You're telling me! thought Floppy.

Chip tried again. 'Doughnuts next, and then I'll take a huge, delicious...bright green rake!' he cried.

Floppy sighed. Why couldn't Chip work it out?

Just then, Jake Blake walked in eating a doughnut. Floppy leapt up and grabbed it out of his hand, then dropped it next to Chip. Jake was cross and stormed out of the room.

Chip looked at the doughnut. 'Oh, I get it,' he said. 'Doughnuts next, and then I'll take a huge, delicious…doughnut break!'

Floppy slumped to the floor. It didn't seem as if Chip was ever going to get it!

Chip tried again. 'A huge, delicious…birthday cake?' he suggested. Floppy barked his approval. At last!

At the baker's, the baker had made an enormous – and rather special – birthday cake, which he put in the shop window. Then Chip, the superintendent, and the baker all hid behind the counter to wait for the robber. They waited . . . and waited . . .

Finally the masked robber burst through the door. 'Doughnuts next, and now I'll take a huge, delicious, birthday cake!' he laughed, greedily.

But just as he stepped towards the cake, Nadim and Floppy jumped out of it, covered in icing. Floppy knocked the robber to the ground and started slurping all the cake off him.

'You're under arrest,' said Nadim, as he handcuffed the robber.

'Good work, Shah, well done, Robinson,' said the Superintendent. 'And I think I know who our rapping robber is!'

Chip pulled off the robber's mask. It was Jake Blake!

'Just as I thought,' the superintendent said grimly. 'Blake, you're a disgrace to the force!'

Jake Blake went red with shame. 'Eating sugar all the time, turned me to a life of crime,' he confessed.

The baker was very pleased. 'Here's a bag of sausage rolls for both of you,' he said to Chip and Nadim.

Floppy was hungry. Wasn't anyone going to give him any food?

'Don't forget my brilliant pet,' said Chip. 'Forget…pet. Hey! That rhymes!'

Chip turned to look at Floppy. 'The key's glowing,' he said.
We're going, thought Floppy.

They were back on the footpath by their school. Chip took out his notepad and pen and started writing furiously. When he'd finished he turned to the others.

'Got it!' he said. They all gathered round as Chip read out his rap.

'Here's a rap about my pet.
He's a dog you won't forget.
He doesn't mind when he's all wet.
Bones are what he likes to get.
He doesn't like to see the vet.
I think he is the best dog yet!'

Everyone clapped and cheered. They all thought it was a brilliant rap – especially Floppy!

OXFORD
UNIVERSITY PRESS

Great Clarendon Street, Oxford OX2 6DP

Oxford University Press is a department of the University of Oxford.
It furthers the University's objective of excellence in research, scholarship,
and education by publishing worldwide in

Oxford New York

Athens Auckland Bangkok Bogotá Buenos Aires Calcutta
Cape Town Chennai Dar es Salaam Delhi Florence Hong Kong Istanbul
Karachi Kuala Lumpur Madrid Melbourne Mexico City Mumbai
Nairobi Paris São Paulo Shanghai Singapore Taipei Tokyo Toronto Warsaw

with associated companies in Berlin Ibadan

Oxford is a registered trade mark of Oxford University Press in the UK and in certain other countries

British Library Cataloguing in Publication Data available
ISBN 0-19-272475-4
1 3 5 7 9 10 8 6 4 2
Printed in Great Britain